LAWYER LOVE

By

Carolyn Gilman Middleton Guyer

Caddie_8@msn.com

14,000 words

Chapter One

Doreen, holding her cheap, old suitcase, walked resolutely down the dusty road. She bought a railroad ticket and clutched it firmly in her hand as she boarded the train for Boston. She was sick of this little run down town and working sunup to sundown and never seeing a penny for it.

"Goodbye, nasty little farm," she whispered out the window as the train chugged along. "I hope I never see you again." A pain pang momentarily choked her when she thought of her parents, but she resolutely put any thought of them aside. The conductor punched her ticket.

The train station was huge and filled with bustling people, knowing where they were going. Doreen went to the cab stand and looked at the first in line. She didn't like his looks and waited for the next taxi to pull forward. Still she waited. When the fifth cab pulled forward, she leaned into the open window and asked the driver if he knew of any inexpensive boarding houses.

He drove her to the South End; must have thought she was Irish; and stopped near a row of houses all looking alike.

"Two dollars," he said, "you will find what you are looking for along here."

She handed him three dollars.

"Thanks," he said, "good luck."

Doreen walked slowly down the street, noting which row house had a room for rent sign and when she got to the crosswalk, turned back. She knocked on the door of the first house.

"I'm inquiring about your room for rent," she told the young girl who answered the door.

The red-haired, freckle-faced girl curtsied to her and said, "Follow me."

She followed up two sets of stairs. The room was small, painted a dull tan, and the window looked out on a dirty alley.

"I was looking for something bigger and in the front of the house," she explained to the gal.

"Try Maude's," the girl said. "Two doors up the street."

"Thank you," she said politely and, after trudging down the stairs, let herself out.

Doreen went two doors, but there was no sign in the window. Maybe she meant the other way, she thought, and traced her steps back. Should she cross the street? She continued on until she saw a rental sign. When she knocked, an older lady answered the door, looked her up and down and stood back for her to enter.

"Are you Maude?" Doreen asked.

"No, I'm Maureen," the woman said. "Follow me."

This time there was only one set of stairs and the room was in the front. It had pretty pink flowers in the wallpaper and the bed was narrow but covered with a nice quilt. The window looked out onto the street.

"How much does it cost?" asked Doreen.

"Twelve dollars a week due on the day you move in. Two weeks required in advance. No cooking; no men visitors; no loud music. Rent includes breakfast at seven am and dinner at six pm. Lunch is your own affair. I change the sheets once a week; provide two towels a week; and you share your bath facilities with two other boarders."

Doreen had no idea if this was a good offer, but she had to stay somewhere until she could get a job. She had enough money for a month; but she was pretty sure she could find employment.

"Let's go to the kitchen and have some tea," the older woman said kindly. "You look like you could use a cuppa and I want one." She smiled sweetly and led Doreen down the stairs and to the back of the house. The kitchen was spotless and Maureen put a teapot on the stove; got out two flowered tea cups and saucers. She put tea in the cups and some cookies on a platter, along with napkins, a creamer, and a sugar bowl. When the water boiled, she poured and added it to the cups and added cream and sugar to her steaming cup.

"Oh, maybe you want lemon," Maureen fussed.

"No thank you," said Doreen, "this is fine."

Maureen asked her where she was from and did she have a job and would she like the room.

Doreen nodded and gave Maureen twenty four dollars. After finishing her tea, she told Maureen she wanted to go to a second hand store.

"It's not far," said Maureen, "I would be glad to go with you. I like to see what other people give away. Don't you?"

The two women walked a few blocks and after crossing the street, turned down a narrow alley where there was a store advertising it was a thrifty store.

Doreen purchased a lamp and two books; a ball of yarn and knitting needles. She looked at a desk, but decided it was too dear.

"I can give you a reduction," said the elderly man behind the counter.

"Do you think we can carry it?" Doreen asked Maureen.

"I will throw in free delivery for tomorrow and take five dollars for it. It has been here forever. You are the only person in Southie who wants a desk," he chuckled.

Doreen gave him her new address. The two women stopped at a grocer and Maureen bought pork chops for dinner and a few vegetables. She told Doreen about the neighborhood and explained how to get around the city by bus and subway. Doreen picked up a newspaper to purchase, but Maureen stopped her and told her she had one at home.

When they arrived home, Maureen put the purchases away and Doreen went to her room to wash up. After putting her meager belongings in the wardrobe and setting up her lamp next to the area where she would put her desk,

Maureen asked her where she was from and did she have a job and would she like the room.

Doreen nodded and gave Maureen twenty four dollars. After finishing her tea, she told Maureen she wanted to go to a second hand store.

"It's not far," said Maureen, "I would be glad to go with you. I like to see what other people give away. Don't you?"

The two women walked a few blocks and after crossing the street, turned down a narrow alley where there was a store advertising it was a thrifty store.

Doreen purchased a lamp and two books; a ball of yarn and knitting needles. She looked at a desk, but decided it was too dear.

"I can give you a reduction," said the elderly man behind the counter.

"Do you think we can carry it?" Doreen asked Maureen.

"I will throw in free delivery for tomorrow and take five dollars for it. It has been here forever. You are the only person in Southie who wants a desk," he chuckled.

Doreen gave him her new address. The two women stopped at a grocer and Maureen bought pork chops for dinner and a few vegetables. She told Doreen about the neighborhood and explained how to get around the city by bus and subway. Doreen picked up a newspaper to purchase, but Maureen stopped her and told her she had one at home.

When they arrived home, Maureen put the purchases away and Doreen went to her room to wash up. After putting her meager belongings in the wardrobe and setting up her lamp next to the area where she would put her desk,

Doreen went downstairs. She found Maureen starting dinner and she voluntarily worked beside her.

Doreen heard a door open and close and her landlady said, "That's Sam Collins. You can set your watch by him. He works in a bank; eats like a horse. He wants his meal at exactly six; very picky, but nice enough. Maybe he knows where you can get a job."

They continued with dinner preparation. Doreen learned where the dishes were and set the large dining room table. There was a lovely lace tablecloth and a vase of flowers.

"Nice," thought Doreen. "I think I will like it here."

After dinner, she cleared the table and started the dishes.

"You don't have to do this," said Maureen.

"Habit," said Doreen. "I don't mind, but I am tired." After everything was tidy, she said good night and went to her room.

After she washed up in the cramped, little bathroom, she put on her nightgown and knelt by the bedside.

"Dear Lord," she prayed, "Thank you for this blessed day and leading me to this kind lady. God bless this house and keep us safe. Amen."

She was asleep as soon as her head hit the pillow.

Chapter two

Doreen was down early and went to the kitchen to help Maureen. She insisted that Doreen sit down and have a cuppa and a nice gossip. Maureen told her about the four boarders she had met the night before. Mr. Gil works in a retail store that sold women's clothing and Miss Fanny works in a tailor shop. "Isn't that strange?" giggled Maureen – "Should be the tother way round. Mr. Collins is a bank teller and Miss Adelia is a maid at a hotel. They will stay a while and then they will be gone."

A young lady with dark hair and red cheeks bustled in the back door.

"Well hello there," she said. "Ma, we have a new one by the looks. I'm Lucinda and help Ma here." She held out her hand and Doreen shook it. Doreen noticed that her nails were painted and she wore lipstick and rouge. She was pretty and her hair had been cut and styled recently. When she took off her coat, Doreen saw her protruding stomach and realized there would be a baby before too long.

"This is Doreen," said Maureen.

"I don't think she looks like a Doreen," said Lucinda. "I think I will call you Dorrie. Where are you working?"

"I just got to the city yesterday," Dorrie said softly. "I will find work real soon."

"Now, Ma," Lucinda said turning to her mother, "I told you a dozen times don't be renting to those unemployed. I work in a salon that helps ladies look better."

Doreen got the impression that Lucinda didn't think she looked too fancy and that being unemployed was a sin.

Maureen's lips were pinched and she asked Dorrie to set the dining room table. Dorrie was only too glad to leave the kitchen.

Lucinda and Maureen ate with Miss Fanny, Dorrie and Mr. Gil and when the boarders bustled off to work, Dorrie helped Maureen clear the table and wash the dishes. Dorrie picked up the newspaper on the kitchen table and turned to the want ads. She found a few ads for typist and borrowing a pencil circled them. Lucinda left without a farewell to Dorrie, but gave her mum a cheek kiss.

Maureen gave Dorrie directions to find the circled places where she might find employment and added that if she were a good typist, she should apply at City Hall. They were always looking for help. She told Dorrie to take extra coins along in case she got lost on the subway and wished her luck.

Dorrie retrieved her old worn coat; after fixing her hair and pinching her lips and cheeks. When she looked in the mirror, she saw a simple woman, not pretty, but not bad looking, with intelligent eyes.

At the first office, the lady at the front desk told her the job was filled. At the second office, a man was at the desk, and lazily showed her to a side office where there was a typewriter and paper.

"Type this until I say stop," said the man. He handed her a page with a story about a bus driver and his passengers.

Dorrie typed for a long time and was wondering if the man had forgotten her. She finished the story and started over.

"I wonder what I did to get her all flustered," Dorrie thought. She was getting very nervous and was thinking she just might leave.

When the woman returned, she said, "My name is Mrs. Greer. Please follow me."

They walked through a maze of cubicles, most with busy young women typing. When they reached the far end, Mrs. Greer knocked on a door. A deep voice said, "Come in," and the two women did so. Mrs. Greer put Dorrie's application and typing test in front of the man and left.

"Thank you Mrs. Greer," Dorrie said politely, just before the door closed.

She turned her attention to the man behind the desk. He was young but older than she was; dressed in an obviously expensive gray suit with a starched white shirt and a tie with a subdued pattern on it. As he studied her paperwork, she looked around the office. The furniture was placed well and besides his desk and her chair; there was a settee and chairs around a small table. There were no files on his desk. The bookcase behind him was filled with law books and pamphlets from floor to ceiling. Dorrie wished she could sit at the table and read some of the books.

"When can you start?" the handsome man asked her abruptly.

"Now?" stammered Dorrie.

The man stared at her. "Please come in next Monday at eight am; ask for Mrs. Greer and she will get you settled in."

"Thank you, Mr. er, uh, what's your name?" she blurted out.

He picked up a letterhead on his desk and pointed to the heading. It read Shingly and Fronts. "I am Shingly," he said. He pushed a button near his phone and Mrs. Greer appeared instantly. She led Dorrie back through the maze and when they reached her office, she gave Dorrie some pamphlets and told her to read them thoroughly before Monday. She advised Dorrie to be timely as Mr. Shingly was annoyed if one was late.

Dorrie left the building before she realized she hadn't asked how much the pay was and what hours and days she was expected to work.

"Oh Dorrie," she said to herself, "You are such an idiot."

Maureen was sipping tea at the kitchen table and was very excited when Dorrie gave her the good news.

"Shingly and Fronts," said Maureen admiringly, "They are one of the best law firms in the city. Look at this," and handed Dorrie an article from the paper. "They are trying a very important case; a doctor is being accused of killing his wife. They represent the doctor."

Dorrie read the article twice.

"Maybe we should go shopping," Maureen suggested quietly. Dorrie realized that she probably didn't look fancy enough for that office.

"Okay," said Dorrie.

They had a grand afternoon and returned tired, but satisfied with time well spent. Dorrie, with Maureen's keen eye, had purchased matching outfits so she could stretch her meager wardrobe. Lucinda arrived shortly after they did and when they told her the good news, she insisted on trimming Dorrie's hair and showing her how to make the best of her features with makeup. Dorrie liked the new look and was glad to have made friends with Lucinda.

Dorrie couldn't wait for the week to end.

Chapter three

Dorrie was up early and so nervous she couldn't eat breakfast. She arrived at the office fifteen minutes early. The doorman greeted her with a smile.

"My name is Edgar," he said. "Do you need directions?"

"I am to meet Mrs. Greer."

"I don't believe she has arrived yet."

"I'll just wait outside her door."

Dorrie stood in the hallway feeling slightly foolish and wondering if she had the time wrong or something. When she heard someone coming up the stairs, she felt relief until she saw it was Mr. Shingly. There was no place to hide.

"Good morning," he said sharply, looking her up and down.

"He is so handsome," Dorrie thought. "Good morning, Mr. Shingly."

Mrs. Greer came up the stairs. She looked startled to see her boss and new protégé standing in the hall. She unlocked her door and invited Dorrie into her office. Mr. Shingly continued down the hallway.

After filling out paperwork on insurance and taxes; receiving a copy of rules and keys to the office, Mrs. Greer showed her to her cubicle. Along the way, she introduced Dorrie to other members of the firm and Dorrie concentrated on remembering names and faces. Stuart, the office boy, brought her supplies: pencils, pens, stenographer books, typing paper, copy paper, tape, correction fluid and a coffee cup with the firm's logo. Stuart asked her to sign her name at the bottom of the list indicating she had received everything. After verifying the supplies, Dorrie arranged them neatly in the drawers of her desk. The chair was hard and uncomfortable, but Dorrie sat quietly and waited for someone to tell her what to do next. She checked out the typewriter and looked at the telephone.

Several women walked by and some smiled shyly at her, but no one spoke.

After an hour, Mrs. Greer appeared.

"Come," she said abruptly.

"Yes ma'am." And Dorrie followed her to Mr. Shingly's office.

Dorrie sat quietly with her pen and stenographer's pad. Mr. Shingly spent the next hour giving Dorrie directions and files with instructions. She carefully made notes of every action she needed to complete.

"When you finish," he said, rising and gathering his briefcase, "leave everything on my desk – here, in this corner."

She returned to her cubicle and arranged her work as he had given it to her. She worked steadily and efficiently until a pretty girl looked over the division from the next office and said, "It's time for lunch. We get thirty minutes. I'm May. I bring my own lunch, but some of the girls go out."

Dorrie said, "I'm Dorrie. All I want is a cup of tea."

"Okay," May responded, "Come with me."

She led her to a small closet with a scarred table and four unmatched chairs. There was a coffee pot and a burner on the shelf. May filled a teapot and boiled water. She filled her own cup with coffee.

May took a brown bag from her large purse and neatly placed a sandwich on a napkin. She ate very slowly and talked between bites. May lived in the South End, also, and she had a boyfriend who worked on the docks. They were planning on wedding in the fall and May said she was saving every penny. She lived at home with her Mum and four younger siblings. Dorrie didn't offer much information about herself, but listened carefully to May's comments and suggestions, as she sipped her tea slowly. Dorrie decided she would talk to Maureen about providing a small lunch; leftovers would be good.

When she returned to her desk, she found Mrs. Greer standing there.

"We are a large law firm," she began "And we have very influential and important clients. You have left your files on your desk – right out in the open where anyone passing through could see them. This is a breach of protocol and will not be tolerated. Do you understand?"

"Yes, ma'am," said Dorrie, turning red in the face. "Is there a special place to leave them?"

"In your desk, and lock it." Mrs. Greer commanded.

Mrs. Greer turned and marched down the area between the cubicles.

Dorrie wanted to cry. What would it look like if she got fired the first day?

The afternoon passed quickly and when Dorrie had finished the work; she put appropriate notes on each file showing what she had done. She took all the files and placed them on Mr. Shingly's desk in the area he had pointed out. She returned to her desk and sat quietly. Dorrie wished she had a watch and wondered how much time there was left.

May popped up over the division and said "It's time to leave. Come along."

Dorrie arrived home just in time for dinner and quietly and quickly ate. The food was good and the conversation of the other boarders calmed her. They all inquired about her first day and seemed genuinely interested, but she said simply it had been a long day.

After helping Maureen clear up and clean up, and arranged for a small lunch Dorrie could take with her the next day, Dorrie asked about the cost; Maureen said her help was enough pay.

Dorrie slept poorly, tossing and turning. She dreamt that Mrs. Greer fired her.

Chapter four

Dorrie said good morning to several of the women and sat at her desk waiting for someone to tell her what to do.

May's head popped up over the division.

"Where are your files?" she hissed, nodding at Mrs. Greer stomping down their way.

"I put them on Mr. Shingly's desk," she whispered back.

"You aren't supposed to do that until you finish them."

"I did," Dorrie said, but May's head had disappeared.

Mrs. Greer stopped at Dorrie's desk. "Mr. Shingly wants to see you." She said grimly.

Dorrie gathered her steno book and walked quickly to Mr. Shingly's office. She tapped on the door and entered. Mrs. Greer followed.

Mr. Shingly stood at the window with his arms behind his back.

Without turning, he said, "We do not allow our employees to spend the night in the office. " He turned slowly and he looked very angry.

Dorrie said startled, "What?"

"Do you speak English?" he continued. "We DO NOT allow our women to spend the night here. We DO NOT run a sweat shop."

"I am – er – sorry, but I don't know what you are talking about," Dorrie stammered.

Mr. Shingly pointed at the pile of files Dorrie had placed on his desk.

Dorrie just stared at him.

"Didn't I do the files correctly?" she asked. She blinked back tears. "I took very good notes and was careful. Which ones did I do wrong? I can correct them quickly."

Mr. Shingly stared at her.

"Do NOT tell me you finished a week's work in one day!" he roared. "Do NOT tell me that!"

Dorrie raised her head and yelled, "You gave me work and I did it. I didn't know I was supposed to take a week to do it." She stomped her foot. "Don't yell at me."

Mr. Shingly and Dorrie faced off across the desk.

Dorrie heard a chuckle from Mrs. Greer. "Well, Alex," she smiled. "I think you have met your match. Good work, Dorrie. Go to your desk; I will be by shortly with your assignment."

When Dorrie saw the other workers leave for lunch, she carefully locked the files in her desk and went to the closet room. She arranged her lunch on a napkin and she fixed a cup of tea. She ate slowly. May did not appear, but Mrs. Greer did. She poured a cup of coffee and said, "That is the closest you will ever come to getting an apology. He's tough, but he's fair. You can go far, if you continue on the same path."

Dorrie nodded at her as she left.

"Mrs. Greer," she called. As the stern lady turned back to her, Dorrie continued, "I don't have a watch or a clock to tell me what time to come or go. Is there one in the supply room, I could borrow until I purchase one?"

She nodded and left.

Stuart, the office boy, brought her a wind up clock with fancy, red flowers and ticking softly. She thanked him and smiled at him. "Don't spend the night," he laughed.

Dorrie blushed. "Does everyone know what happened?"

"This place is a gossip pit. Mr. Shingly has a loud voice when he's angry."

When he left, May looked over the division.

"I can't believe he apologized to you," she said. "He never comes through here."

Dorrie didn't answer her and worked diligently all afternoon. She locked the files in her desk and left. May didn't offer to walk with her to the bus stop.

When she shared with Maureen what had happened; Maureen praised her for sticking up for herself and for working with Mr. Shingly.

"He is one of the city's most eligible bachelors. He's always in the paper and has a different lady on his arm. See?" She continued by handing her a section of the paper that dealt with the social news. There was a picture of Alex dancing with a beautiful blonde.

Mr. Shingly continued to call her every morning and assign work to her. She continued to do the work quickly, and with a minimum of mistakes. Her life took on a boring routine, but satisfying. Her first paycheck was for forty-five dollars and she was amazed. I can make it, she thought. I can live on this.

The other workers stayed aloof, and while she remained friends with May, none of the others paid her any attention or invited her to lunch or said more than good morning. When she took the matter up with Maureen, her advice was to be friendly but aloof too.

"They are jealous because you work for Mr. Shingly exclusively. They have been there longer and just available to whoever needs some typing. You should be proud you have advanced so quickly."

It was true, thought Dorrie. She felt better about her feelings and proud of her accomplishments. When she knelt that night to say her evening prayers, she thanked God gratefully. Life was calm; like a still lake.

Chapter five

Once a month Mrs. Greer had a meeting in the Board Room where she gave out assignments; made announcements; and generally let everyone know of changes. She seldom asked anyone to speak and everyone complained behind her back; therefore, everyone was surprised when she announced that Mr. Shingly would address them.

When he entered the Board Room, he wore a well-tailored black suit, his traditional starched white shirt and a striped tie. Dorrie looked around the room and saw several of the women gazing at him as though he was a delicious piece of candy. She had the sudden urge to laugh and bit her lip.

"As you may know," he began, "I take part in a number of charities and fund raisers. This next weekend is no exception and on Saturday evening, I will be attempting to make some elite Bostonians give me money for a worthy cause; always a difficult job." The girls smiled.

"I thought that it would be a nice touch to invite one of you to attend with me." The girls all sat up and gasped. It was obvious that any one of them would be thrilled to go.

"If you would please write your name on a piece of paper and give it to Mrs. Greer, I will draw out a name. My "date" will be given one hundred dollars for an appropriate gown and a day off to get prepared. Good luck to you all."

Mrs. Greer held out a bowl with the names in it.

"And the winner is," Mr. Shingly said picking out a paper, "Dorrie Dustin."

Dorrie sat in shock. She couldn't do this; go on a date with her boss; talk to all those ritzy people; get dressed up;

and actually talk to him. The other girls exchanged glances and some muttering was heard. Dorrie thought they probably believed it was fixed.

The meeting ended with the workers filing out quietly. No one congratulated Dorrie. She returned to her cubicle and worked through lunch and left at her usual time without a word to anyone. Even May had stopped popping up.

Maureen was so happy for her and hugged her.

"You will be beautiful and have a great time," she said. "I bet you even get your picture in the paper. Wait until I tell Lucinda; she will be green with envy."

Maureen and Dorrie rode the bus to downtown Boston and spent Dorrie's day off shopping and gazing at all the beautiful gowns. They finally settled on a simple turquoise dress with small straps over the shoulders. It fell in gentle folds to the ground and it cost more money than Dorrie had spent in her entire life. When she hesitated, Maureen urged her on by telling her this was a once in a lifetime opportunity and she should make the most of it. They picked out some nice high heels, a small evening bag, and some undergarments meant to be worn with a gown of this ilk. When they returned home, Lucinda was sitting in the kitchen sipping coffee. Maureen showed her all the wonderful purchases and talked incessantly about the fashions they had seen. Lucinda admired it all.

"I will be here at five tomorrow," Lucinda said, "to do your hair and makeup. I have just the right idea." Dorrie was grateful and thanked Lucinda.

The big evening had arrived. Dorrie was stunning in the simple gown and Lucinda had styled her hair in a becoming fashion. She had added a large shiny barrette to her hair that was just the right touch. Dorrie couldn't believe the mirror image was her – she really looked good!

A limousine arrived at eight o'clock sharp and a driver knocked on the door.

"Miss Dustin's car has arrived," he announced.

Dorrie entered the car and waved happily to the boarders, Maureen and Lucinda who were all gathered on the steps. She admired the lovely interior of the car. The driver drove with care and they soon arrived at the Ball Room. When the driver opened her door, Mr. Shingly stepped forward and gave Dorrie his hand to help her from the car.

"What has happened to my mousy little typist? Did her fairy godmother turn her into Cinderella?" he teased.

He was dressed in a black and white tuxedo and his hair had been cut recently. Dorrie thought he smelled really good.

"You make a fine prince," she teased back.

They walked up the cement stairs. Dorrie was nervous and hoped she wouldn't be embarrassed by tripping, but she made it to the top without accident. Photographers snapped pictures of her boss and asked her name.

Dorrie was introduced over and over to some of the richest people in Boston and was careful to talk nicely and listen attentively. There were numerous speakers requesting donations for the cause. Dinner was chicken, rather dry, salad and mixed vegetables which were over cooked. Dorrie hardly touched her meal. She drank some wine; something she had never done. It was sweet and tasted okay; she began to relax.

"Let's dance," said Mr. Shingly, taking her hand and pulling her forward.

Dorrie had not considered this particular event and pulled back.

"Mr. Shingly," she said quietly, "I don't know how to dance."

"First," he said, "call me Alex when we are out of the office and second, you just follow my lead."

He pulled her onto the dance floor.

"Don't look at your feet," he ordered.

He held her in a waltz position and stepped lightly onto the floor. She had no choice but to follow. After a few turns, Dorrie realized it was easy and really began to enjoy herself. Her eyes shone and she looked around at the other dancers who seemed to be enjoying themselves also.

He pulled her closer and they whirled around the room in unison. "Wow," thought Dorrie, "This is fun!"

"You smell good," she blurted out. Immediately, she blushed at her insane comment.

After a slight pause, Alex threw back his head and laughed heartily.

"I am so glad you approve, my little mouse," he whispered. He twirled her out of the room, through double glass doors and onto a stone veranda overlooking well-appointed gardens complete with water falls, flowers and statues. Dorrie wondered if he had drunk too much; he was so different from the office.

Gently, he took her chin and raised her face, kissing her lips softly.

"Ah-h-h" he sighed, "I knew it."

"Knew what?" asked Dorrie

"That your lips are soft; that you are a rare gem; and that we would get along fabulously."

When he leaned forward for another kiss, Dorrie said, "I would like to dance some more; that is so much fun." He obligingly returned to the dance floor and after a few more rounds suggested they get some punch.

"Good idea," said Dorrie. "I wish I could stick my feet in the fountain; they are killing me."

Again, Alex threw back his head and laughed heartily. A nearby photographer snapped a picture and then another as Dorrie and Alex touched foreheads, smiling.

They took their drinks to the table and sat talking. Alex asked her about her life and where she wanted to go with it. He pulled his chair close and put his arm around her shoulder. He leaned in attentively as Dorrie talked more than she had in a long time; telling him things she knew she probably shouldn't but couldn't refrain. She blamed it on the punch.

The limousine driver seemed surprised to see Alex but quickly masked his face not to reveal his feelings. Alex had never seen any of his dates home to his knowledge. He looked closer at Dorrie, but she was just another pretty face to him. He drove slowly, taking the long way.

Dorrie and Alex had a champagne drink; a first for Dorrie. It was bubbly and tickled her nose, making her laugh. She had a cute giggle and Alex smiled fondly at her.

"I really like this girl - uh – woman," he thought.

He leaned towards her, kissing her lips. He increased the pressure and drew her closer. He could feel her small breasts against his chest and he put his hands on her face as she drew away.

"Do you have a boyfriend?" he asked narrowing his eyes.

"Absolutely not," she answered. "But I definitely like your kissing."

He laughed. "And I like you kissing me back."

They had some more champagne and the driver, made a wrong turn and went well out of his way. His passengers didn't even notice.

She had never been kissed so much. It was exhilarating and thrilling. He told her funny stories from work and serious stories about his family. She was entranced.

He walked her to the front door and kissed her again and again.

"Do you like living here?" he asked.

"Yes, very much." She answered.

He looked thoughtful. She told him what a wonderful time and how she enjoyed it. He thanked her for the evening and left.

Maureen was in the kitchen.

"You were peeking out the window, weren't you?" accused Dorrie laughing.

"Of course," Maureen said, "Oh my, he is handsome. You looked like you were enjoying all those kisses."

"Oh yes," Dorrie said. "I drank champagne and danced and kissed and the dinner was horrid – dried chicken and squishy vegetables. I hate squishy vegetables."

Maureen said, "I think you are half smashed."

"Oh yes," said Dorrie, "I am sure you are right. I'm famished; any food left over?"

Maureen fixed her a bowl of beef stew, served with warmed over biscuits. It was delicious.

"I don't believe I will sleep a wink," said Dorrie.

She wasn't in bed a minute before the lights went out. She was awakened by Maureen banging on her door.

"Get up, Dorrie, get up," she called through the door. "Come here, quickly."

Dorrie jumped out of bed, thinking something was terribly wrong, and throwing the quilt around her, opened the door.

Maureen grabbed her by the hand and pulled her downstairs. On the kitchen table was a beautiful bouquet of flowers with a card attached. It read: I had the most enjoyable evening ever, Alex. Dorrie admired the flowers but privately thought he probably did this for all his dates and didn't think she was special. Maureen fixed her a cup of coffee with lots of cream and sugar and then handed her the newspaper, folded to the social section. Dorrie stared at Alex laughing at a beautiful woman who smiled shyly. The next picture was Alex dancing again with the same woman. The third picture showed them kissing on the veranda.

"When did he have time for all that?" thought Dorrie. Then she looked closer.

"Oh my goodness!" she exclaimed. "That can't be me, can it?"

Lucinda rushed in. "Did you see the paper, Ma? Dorrie, you are gorgeous!! You were kissing and he is so handsome!!"

Dorrie's head felt like a little man with a pile driver was working hard.

Maureen gave her two pills and some more coffee.

The women continued to exclaim over the article. They took turns reading it to her and admiring the pictures.

Dorrie's only thought was how she was going to face the office women and him on Monday.

Chapter five

To Dorrie's relief, Alex had left for court, and she wouldn't have to face him; however, Mrs. Greer rang her and asked her to come to her office at ten.

May came around to the cubicle opening and leaned against the wall. Dorrie could feel all the women become attentive to their conversation.

"Saw you in the paper," said May. She sounded pouty. "I saw all the pictures."

"Don't believe everything you read or see," said Dorrie loudly. "Newspapers like to exaggerate and doctor those pictures. It really wasn't like that."

May had a puzzled look on her face. "Oh," she said. "Then you didn't kiss him?"

"Of course not," lied Dorrie indignantly, "He's my boss. I hardly saw him all evening."

"I told the girls it didn't look like you at all." May said, obviously relieved.

A girl named Sally Ann who sat directly across from Dorrie and had never spoken to her, came to stand by May.

"Did you have a good time?" she asked

"Oh yes, but the food was horrid; dried chicken and squishy vegetables. You would think a place that fancy would have better cooks. The music was dreamy but I don't really know how to dance."

Another worker named Stella, came by and said, "If you want to learn how to dance, I can teach you. Me and my beau go dancing at a nightclub every weekend. I love dancing."

"I doubt if I get another chance, but that's so sweet," said Dorrie. "Mrs. Greer wants to see me at ten – do you think I'm fired?"

The women looked anxious and finally Stella said "I hope not." She sounded insincere.

At ten, Dorrie knocked on Mrs. Greer's door which was answered immediately by a sharp "come in."

"Mr. Shingly has been very impressed with your work ethic and your demeanor." She began with no preamble. She motioned to a chair. "He is, however, concerned that you are not being challenged to your full capacity. Do you know what a law clerk is?"

She didn't wait for an answer. "A law clerk is someone studying to be a lawyer and to further his studies, attaches himself to a law firm to run errands, file motions and do much of the research for current cases. Mr. Shingly has suggested that we subsidize your enrollment in law school and hire you as a law clerk until you become a full-fledged lawyer."

Dorrie's mouth dropped open.

"I don't expect you to make an immediate decision, of course," she continued. "You may have a week to decide. I have never heard of a female law clerk and very few female lawyers. You will have a hard time and many lawyers will look at you as an impostor. Your fellow typists will assume you are sleeping your way to this position. I do not want this proposition bandied around the typing pool and if you decide to take this amazing opportunity, Mr. Shingly and I will handle all announcements. That is all."

"Did you get fired?" May whispered over the division top.

"No," said Dorrie, "something else altogether."

Dorrie did not see Mr. Shingly until Friday afternoon when he returned from court. He called her into his office. The moment the door closed, Mr. Shingly grabbed Dorrie and pushing her against the door, proceeded to kiss her thoroughly.

Dorrie dropped her stenographer's pad and pencil and kissed him back – thoroughly.

"Oh, I've missed you so," whispered Alex.

"I thought you were avoiding me," said Dorrie.

"Never," Alex said nibbling at her ear. "My driver will pick you up at eight tonight and we will go out to dinner. I have so much to tell you. Do you have a curfew?"

"A what?" said Dorrie.

"Where you live – do you have to be home at a certain time?"

"I have no idea; I have never been out."

Alex gave her a strange look and said, "Well, tonight you have a hot date."

Dorrie smiled.

True to his word, Alex's driver knocked on the door at eight, and handed Dorrie into his limo. She had dressed in a casual flowered print dress and her slippers because she had no idea what one wore on a "hot date."

Maureen said she locked the door at midnight and Dorrie said she was sure she would be home by then.

The driver whisked her quickly through the narrow streets of Boston and stopped before a small Italian restaurant in the North End. Alex was leaning against the wall beside the front door and came forward to help Dorrie from the car. He kissed her hand.

"What time, boss," asked the driver.

"We'll take a taxi," Alex said. "You can have the night off."

"My missus will sure appreciate that. Thank you." And he drove away.

The room was small with red table cloths and candles in wine bottles. It was slightly dingy, but smelled delicious.

Alex led her through the room and pushed open a door to a smaller room, one with a table for two, white table cloth and the traditional wine bottle candles.

"I hope you like Italian food." Alex said, holding her chair out for her.

"I don't know," said Dorrie. "I can't ever remember eating it. Well, I've had pizza."

Alex chuckled. "I am going to give you an education; a full education in everything. This is so much fun."

Dorrie answered, "I am a quick learner."

"I noticed the very first week. I still can't believe how fast you work and how efficient. I think you are an alien from another planet or you sleep at the office."

Dorrie laughed. "Silly, I would never get any sleep in that horrid chair I have. It is like a cement bench."

"Well, as of Monday, your office will be next to mine; and I will make sure you have a comfortable chair. On Tuesdays and Thursdays, you will go to the law college, taking six classes at a time. I'm sure you can handle that. Mrs. Greer has your schedule. On Monday, Wednesday and

Friday you will work in your new office. You will be looking up precedents and laws I can use in court. Of course, any of the firm's lawyers can use you, but hopefully you will be exclusively mine. On Saturdays and Sundays, you belong to me as I educate you in other matters – like kissing," he said. He bent forward and kissed her soundly.

"Oh, I do like kissing you." Dorrie said. "But you haven't given me a chance to refuse. What if I can't do it?"

"Silly girl," he said. "You can't refuse. I won't let you and of course you can do it. It's simple when you have your boss for reference and guidance. And one more thing: your salary will double as of Monday; your college and books are all paid for and I think you should move."

"That's three things," Dorrie said mischievously. A waiter stepped forward and filled their wine glasses.

"Move? But why? I like Maureen and my little room." She sipped her wine. "I can get use to this," she thought.

"Well, you will be very busy and if you lived nearer the college, which is also nearer to the office and the courthouse, you will spend less time running to the South End. I have several suggestions."

"I live with my mother on Beacon Hill," he continued. "We live totally separate lives and seldom see each other, but I don't think you should move in with us. It would cause a great scene and lots of gossip." He laughed to show he was joking. "There are several small apartments near me and I would like to spend tomorrow with you, examining them. What do you think?"

Alex noticed how pale Dorrie looked and immediately became solicitous, taking her hand and turning it over, kissed her palm. He ran his tongue across her palm.

Dorrie couldn't think straight. Strange feelings were racing through her entire body.

"Everything is moving too quickly," she whispered, feeling very confused and upset.

"If you are on a merry-go-round, you must grab the gold ring quickly," Alex said. "Just let yourself go."

"I've never been on a merry-go-round," Dorrie said sadly.

"Let go," said Alex simply. "Let go and we will forget everything except how much we like each other."

"Good idea," said Dorrie. "Please order for me since I might end up with snail's bellies or cat's brains if I did."

Alex let out his loud laugh that Dorrie loved. They ate and drank and talked incessantly about everything but work and the new chapter of Dorrie's life. When they were finished, Dorrie and Alex walked hand in hand down the sidewalk to a downstairs jazz club. They danced and danced and laughed and drank. The music was really good: Dorrie decided she loved the saxophone.

"Last call," the waitress announced.

"One more?" asked Alex.

"I've had enough, actually, too much," laughed Dorrie. "What time is it?"

"You need a watch," said Alex. "It's just past midnight."

"Oh, no," Dorrie said in distress, "Maureen locks the door at twelve."

"Well, we will take her a present and wake her up," Alex said as he ordered a bottle of wine to go. He hailed a taxi. The driver was reluctant to go to the South End, but Alex persuaded him with a large bill.

"What's wrong with the South End?" asked Dorrie. "I like it there."

Alex answered by taking her in his arms and kissing her thoroughly.

The taxi sped away and Alex rang the doorbell. The door opened almost immediately and Maureen stood there in her worn bathrobe and curlers in her hair.

"Maureen," Alex said, "my name is Alex Shingly and I found this wayward girl hanging on the street corner. Does she belong to you?"

Maureen had obviously going to give Dorrie a tongue lashing, but ended up laughing instead. Dorrie grinned. Alex certainly had a way with women.

"Peace offering," Alex said, holding out the bottle of wine. "Show me the glasses," and he pushed by her and found his way to the kitchen. Maureen raised an eyebrow at Dorrie.

"And how much did you two drink already?" asked Maureen caustically. She took Dorrie's arm and led her crookedly to the kitchen where she put on the coffee pot.

"Good idea," said Alex and put the wine on the shelf unopened.

The three of them drank coffee and ate some pie that Maureen had made the day before. Alex explained the firm's offer to Maureen, praising Dorrie often.

Maureen hugged Dorrie. "You have no idea what a fine employee you have here," she bragged to Alex. "She will do you proud. Lucinda lives on Beacon Hill."

Dorrie looked surprised. "I didn't know that."

Maureen shrugged, "all the big wigs live there and now you will be one of them. Just don't forget your old friend."

Dorrie had tears in her eyes as she laid her head on Maureen's shoulder.

Alex called a cab and when the driver tooted, Alex kissed Dorrie thoroughly.

"Good night, sweetheart," he said, and was gone.

"The minute I laid eyes on you, I knew you were destined for great things," said Maureen proudly. "I am so happy for you."

The next morning Dorrie and Maureen worked feverishly to get all the chores done and when Alex rang to say he would pick her up around one to look at the apartments he had chosen, they were almost done for the day.

They sat quietly sipping tea.

"Are you sure you want me to go?" asked Maureen for the umpteenth time. "Maybe Mr. Singly wants to be alone with you."

"Poppycock," laughed Dorrie. "If you don't go, I don't go."

"You are right," laughed Maureen, "you might not be able to control yourself if you are alone with him in an empty apartment. I am not pulling splinters from your hind end."

They were giggling uncontrollable, holding their tummies; tears streaming down their faces, when Alex walked in the room. No matter how much he tried, he could not find out what was so funny.

The two women looked over each of the three apartments carefully, discussing pros and cons. They talked about furniture and draperies and finally decided on which apartment and Maureen said she would oversee the decorations, stating that Dorrie was a "bookworm" and didn't know damask from calico.

"That's true," said Dorrie sadly.

Alex poked her in the ribs and made her laugh. The three good friends went to a sandwich shop and had lunch.

"I can't remember the last time I ate out," said Maureen. "This is so much fun."

Alex dropped them off at the front door, dropping a kiss on Maureen's cheek which made her blush and kissed Dorrie firmly on her lips.

As Alex's driver took him away, Lucinda rushed from the house, red faced and angry.

"Ma," she yelled, "What are you doing? Riding in limousines? Kissing on the street? Are you crazy? This is all your doing," she ranted, turning on Dorrie. "I knew when I saw you, you were no good and trouble, trouble, trouble!"

Maureen said sharply, "That's enough Lucinda June O'Toole Gibson."

Lucinda stomped off.

"I am so sorry," Doreen said for the twentieth time.

"It's not your fault," Maureen said sadly. "My husband Amos, he spoiled her rotten; gave her anything she wanted."

Doreen picked up her room and packed what she was taking and putting the rest in a box for Maureen. She looked sadly at the desk where she had spent many hours reading, but decided not to take it.

"I will miss you," she said to the room.

Chapter six

On Monday, Dorrie didn't know where to go. Should she go to her new office or to her cubicle or to Mrs. Greer's office? When Edgar opened the glass doors for her, he said, "Welcome to your new job." Dorrie smiled and thanked him happily. Before the door closed, Mrs. Greer entered.

"Come with me," she said to Dorrie. When they got to Mrs. Greer's office, she unlocked the door and desk and took out some keys, which she handed to Dorrie. "This is to the office and this is to the backdoor. Most of the lawyers come through the back door which is kept locked. They don't want to meet any of their clients unexpectedly." She walked with Dorrie and when they passed her old cubicle, Dorrie saw that it was cleaned out. At the new office, Mrs. Greer, stepped aside so Dorrie could unlock the door; telling Dorrie to make a list of things she wanted.

"Thank you, Mrs. Greer," Dorrie said politely.

On the desk was a small bouquet of flowers with a note that said good luck. It wasn't signed but Dorrie was certain it was from Alex. There were school books on the desk and a new briefcase that could hold them. There were files, both empty and full, with a note for Dorrie to review them.

The chair was new and very comfortable.

"Thank you, God," Dorrie prayed.

She spent the day arranging her desk, reviewing files, looking up cases in the library and taking copious notes. At lunchtime, she went to a diner across the street and sat staring out at the busy people. She had a small sandwich and a glass of iced tea. She was happy she could afford this small luxury.

When her little red rose clock said five, she left for the day. Tomorrow she would be a student and she could hardly sleep.

College was very confusing and Dorrie hated confusion. She kept asking how to get to this class and which book she needed and became totally frustrated when she looked at the work due for the next class.

Alex's driver was waiting at the curb. Dorrie was surprised and ran down the steps as he opened the door. Several students stood in awe as the "new student" was rushed away in the limo.

He drove her to her new apartment and went with her to unlock the door. He gave her the keys and asked if she would need anything tonight.

"I don't think so," said Dorrie. "I don't know."

He handed her a card. The number was followed by the name Allen. "You can call me anytime, night or day, for anything." He tipped his hat and left.

Dorrie entered the apartment slowly. She had never lived all alone. She was feeling sorry for herself, until Maureen and Lucinda appeared at the kitchen door.

"Welcome to your new home," they said in unison.

Dorrie fell into their arms and sobbed.

"Well, that's a find thank you," sniffed Lucinda. "After all the work we did all day. And me with this big fellow kicking."

"I miss you so," sobbed Dorrie.

"Pshaw," said Maureen, "How could you miss us when you haven't even been gone twenty-four hours?"

After a cuppa, Maureen and Lucinda proudly showed Dorrie around. They had put up drapes and Alex had arranged for the furniture to be brought. They even had her old desk prominently displayed. The bed was made with new crispy sheets and the kitchen was fully stocked.

"I am so late," said Maureen. "I am going to lose all my boarders."

"Wait," said Dorrie. She dialed Allen's number and he said he would be there in five minutes.

After Maureen kissed Dorrie and hugged Lucinda, she was whisked away to the South End. Lucinda and Dorrie stood on the stoop waving.

"I want to apologize," said Lucinda. "Ever since I got this kid, I have been a witch. I am so sorry,"

"Pshaw," said Dorrie, imitating Maureen, which made them both laugh.

"I only live two streets over," Lucinda said. "This is my number and you can call me if you want something."

Dorrie was overwhelmed with gratitude and hugged her in fond farewell.

Chapter seven

Dorrie woke up and hearing a ringing sound, she sat up. Where was she? The preceding week came to her in a rush. It was the telephone in the kitchen ringing.

"Good morning, Dorrie," said Alex. "How is your new apartment? Is there anything you need?

"I need you," she said sleepily.

There was a long pause.

"How did your classes go?" he finally asked.

"I got lost and I got tons of homework."

"I left work on your desk, but it isn't pressing. Close your office door and study; your boss won't object."

Dorrie laughed. "Are you in the office?"

"No," said Alex. "I am at home. Allen is picking me up in a half hour and we will stop by and pick you up if you can get ready by then."

He sounded so cold; had she done something wrong; was he angry with her for something.

"Okay," she said and hung up.

One of the nicest things about her apartment was a bathroom she didn't share. The water was hot and she took a quick wash-up; dressed in her office clothes and was enjoying a cuppa when the doorbell rang. She grabbed her briefcase full of books; her keys and a sweater. Allen held the door for her and she slid in next to Alex who was reading a brief from a file on his lap.

"Good morning," he said absent mindedly. "How is your new apartment?"

"Wonderful," Dorrie said happily. "Thank you for everything."

"We have an appointment as soon as we get to the office."

"Okay," said Dorrie, wondering what that was about. She hoped she wasn't in trouble. *Why do I worry so?*

Allen let them out at the back door of the building and Dorrie followed Alex. She went to her office and dropped her belongings; then went to Alex's office next door and knocked. Alex and Mrs. Greer and a stranger were in the room, obviously waiting her arrival.

"This is Detective Graham from the New Hampshire State Police," Alex said coldly.

Mrs. Greer said nothing.

Detective Graham said, "I have been hired by Alice and Elias, your parents, to locate you and return you to your home."

Dorrie turned white and her hands were trembling.

"Why?" she finally managed to say.

"Because you ran away, and they have been worried sick about you. They thought you had met with foul play. I am taking you home today."

"Like the dickens you are." Dorrie said. "What are you talking about? I am twenty-three years old. I can go where I want to and when I want to and there is no law in this country that says you can forcibly remove me against my will. My parents are just angry that they don't have a slave to work for them from sunup to sundown for no pay. You can't make me go."

She turned to Alex and added, "Can he? Can he drag me out of here to return me to the nasty little town?"

Alex turned to the State Trooper. "Get out," he said loudly and angrily. "You intimated that Dorrie was wanted. You led me to believe she had broken a law. Get out, you worm," And he held the door open.

Dorrie broke down sobbing bitterly.

Mrs. Greer left the office quietly without speaking.

Alex went to the door and turned the lock; then he took Dorrie in his arms and held her. Neither spoke until Dorrie said, "Oh no, look what I did to your suit."

Alex chuckled. "I keep a spare in the closet here in case some damsel in distress cries all over me."

"Do me a favor," he said still chuckling, "If the Judge throws me in jail for being late, will you please arrange my bail and hire me a lawyer to represent me."

Dorrie giggled. Alex took out his handkerchief and wiped her face.

"If you blow your nose on my handkerchief, don't give it back to me," he said.

Dorrie giggled again and blew her nose loudly.

Alex left, laughing all the way.

Alex never questioned Dorrie about her family and never mentioned the Policeman that had traced Dorrie to him. Mrs. Greer was her same stern self and if she had an opinion, it was never voiced.

Dorrie spent the day studying and working on files and researching cases. At five, she left by the back door and found Allen waiting for her.

"I am going to get fat, if you never let me walk anywhere," she complained to Allen. He smiled.

He drove her to a popular restaurant and said Alex was waiting for her inside. Then he drove away.

Dorrie walked into the room hesitantly, but the hostess immediately called her by name and led her to a private room. Alex rose as she entered and thanked the hostess. Alex was accompanied by a very attractive lady and Dorrie felt a pang of jealousy.

"Dorrie," Alex said proudly, "I want to introduce you to my mother, Mary Shingly. Mother, this is my sweetheart Dorrie."

Mary graciously held out her hand and Dorrie took it just as graciously.

"I am pleased to meet you Mrs. Shingly."

"Oh, no, Dorrie, please call me Mary."

The three companions had drinks and dinner; Alex ordering for Dorrie; and talked quietly about Boston and the wonderful things about the city.

"I understand you are a law clerk," said Mary. "Are you going into law?"

"Yes ma'am," Dorrie said proudly. "I hope Alex will hire me after I graduate. Not many law firms have lady lawyers."

"That's true," said Mary thoughtfully.

"I am holding a small soiree next Saturday evening for a few of my dear friends," she continued. "I would be honored if you would attend with Alex."

"A lot of ladies gossiping," said Alex, "The only way she can get me to one of those is having you there. I won't be upset if you say no."

"I'd love to come," said Dorrie smiling mischievously at Alex.

Alex groaned.

"I can see I am going to be outnumbered for the rest of my life,"

Mary raised her eyebrow and looked closer at Dorrie and then at Alex, but she said nothing. The rest of the meal proceeded with good food and intelligent conversation. Dorrie thoroughly enjoyed herself.

After dessert, a chauffeur entered the room and announced to Mary that he would take her home now. They left after kindly goodbyes.

Alex moved his chair closer and looking deeply into her eyes said, "Let's go to your apartment."

Dorrie was nervous and she had homework to complete. She nodded and soon Allen had whisked them away. Alex told Allen to go home; he would walk. Dorrie had never heard of Alex walking anywhere. She became more nervous.

Alex took the keys from her shaking hand and opened the door. As soon as she entered, he pressed her against the wall, kissing her passionately.

"You don't know how I've missed doing this," he said. "You set me on fire."

Dorrie locked the front door and went to the kitchen. As she put a pot of coffee on the stove to heat, he pulled her back into his arms; kissing her.

They separated only when the coffee pot boiled over making loud sizzling sounds. Dorrie got two cups down and poured coffee. She added milk and sugar. Her hands were shaking and she felt weak. He sat at the table and pulled her into his lap.

"I want you," he whispered. "I really, really want you."

Dorrie squirmed. "I, uh, uh, I have never done this," she said. "I don't know what to do and I feel all funny inside and I like you so much."

Alex pulled away and sipped his coffee.

"Dorrie, my darling," he said, "are you telling me you are a virgin?"

Dorrie blushed. "Yes," she whispered.

Alex stood up abruptly.

He gently took her in his arms and rubbing her back, said, "It's okay Dorrie. I have to get home and you must have studying to do."

Dorrie felt a great let down. She sadly kissed him goodnight and let him out the door. She didn't do her homework for the first time and she cried herself to sleep.

Chapter eight

Dorrie didn't go to Mary's soiree; instead she went to Maureen's and cried on her shoulder. She sobbed until there were no more tears left. Maureen and Dorrie went to the Thrifty Store and Maureen found a book she wanted to read. Dorrie sadly looked over the second-hand goods but didn't see anything that caught her fancy.

Dorrie invited Lucinda and Maureen over for tea the next weekend. Lucinda was too large to go out in public and was anxious to have her baby alive and healthy.

The next week Lucinda had a beautiful baby boy and Dorrie joined Maureen at the hospital to see him. Maureen was thrilled to be a grandmother.

Dorrie worked hard both at the office and at school. She seldom saw Alex and then only from a distance.

Occasionally she saw his picture in the paper with some young, lovely on his arm at a fund raiser or charity event. It made her sad.

Dorrie's finals were hard. A whole year behind her now, she thought as she took the last test.

The following week, Alex left a note on her desk to see him the next day at eight am.

"Probably going to fire me," she grumbled to Maureen and Lucinda that evening. "Just because I am a virgin. Well, I am not sleeping with anyone until I have a wedding ring on my finger, which isn't going to happen. Do you know that one of my professors said that more women weren't lawyers because you had to be a lesbian?"

Lucinda and Maureen stared at her. "He didn't," gasped Lucinda.

"Oh, yes, he did," said Dorrie. "And I am the only woman in his class. Can't get more specific than that, can you?"

"Are you sure you want to keep at this?" asked Maureen. "You can always move back with me and run the house together. I am really feeling tired lately. When these boarders leave, I am not taking any more. It is just too much."

"You can always move with me, Ma," said Lucinda. "I know Harold would love it. He likes your cooking."

"Or move with me," offered Dorrie. "Looks like I am going to die a virgin so I might as well live with a woman. Maybe I am a lesbian and don't know it."

Maureen looked uncomfortable. Lucinda said, "You are not going to have my mother branded a lesbian."

At eight o'clock sharp, Dorrie knocked on Alex's door and went in when he called enter. He was looking particularly handsome in a gray oxford with a yellow and gray tie. Dorrie dropped her eyes and said, "You wanted to see me."

Alex didn't look up. He had several papers in front of him and Dorrie could see the law college's logo on the page.

"Because we are your benefactor," Alex commenced, "the college sends your grades directly to the firm. Do you know what your grades were for the year?"

"No," a subdued Dorrie said.

He handed her a paper. She noticed he trembled a bit and wondered if it was that bad. She read it once; then she read it twice.

"Oh boy," she exclaimed. "Oh boy, this is great." She smiled sweetly at Alex. "You scared me to death. I thought you were getting rid of me. You aren't are you?" she added hesitantly.

"Of course not," he said impatiently. "Because you have the highest grades in your class, you made the Dean's List and you receive this." He showed her a medal hung on a red, white and blue ribbon. He came around the desk and put it over her head, letting it drop between her breasts. She raised her head and his lips sought hers. She was on her feet in an instant, almost knocking him over. She ground her lips into his; she moaned.

Dorrie let go and hurried from his office. She locked her door and wept bitterly. She didn't answer the door when someone knocked. She tried to work, but she couldn't concentrate and finally she rang Mrs. Greer.

"I am not feeling well at all and would like to go home," she told the startled woman.

"Of course you may," Mrs. Greer answered.

And Dorrie went home. She cleaned her apartment and went to the market. She stopped at a pet store window and looked at the puppies and kittens for sale. It would be so nice to have something to love she thought sadly, but went home.

Christmas would be here soon and Dorrie needed to decide what presents to buy. She had accumulated quite a large sum of money thanks to the generosity of the firm. She just didn't know what to buy.

There was an envelope attached to her door with the word Tenant typed across the front. Dorrie dropped her groceries in the kitchen, put on a pot for tea, and sat at the table.

The letter was an official notice from the owner of the building that he would be selling the building and all leases were canceled. When there was a new owner, they would be notified.

Dorrie was horrified. She loved this apartment; it was just the right size; she loved the furniture and the kitchen. Maureen and Lucinda came often and Alex had chosen well. Every time she thought of Alex, she had a pain somewhere in the vicinity of her heart. She wondered what he was doing for Christmas and New Year. She had never heard from Mary again. Even Allen had abandoned her.

The next day, she left a note in Alex's mailbox that she needed to see him at his convenience. Twenty minutes later, a loud knock sounded and Alex banged into her office.

"What's this?" he yelled. "After all we've done for you, you are leaving us? Who do you think you are? You just can't walk away from all this."

Dorrie quietly rose from her chair and closed the door to her office. She could see several of the typists in the pool looking in her direction.

She handed Alex the notice she had received from the current owner of her apartment building. He read it once and then again. He looked very sheepish.

"I thought you should know about this, since this firm put the deposit down for me; bought the furniture and signed the lease on my behalf," she said very professionally.

Alex came around the desk and pulled Dorrie into his arms. "I always have to tell you I am sorry, but this time I am really, really sorry.   We always seem to be misunderstanding each other." His lips sought hers. They were soft and warm and Dorrie had missed his lips on hers. She returned his kiss lightly and then pulled back.

"I know this firm has been very good to me. I know you have gone out of the way to see some of my fondest dreams come true. I wanted one more favor and then I won't ask for more." She paused. "Would the firm buy the building? I don't want to move."

"Let's have dinner tonight," Alex said. "Maybe at the Italian restaurant; I haven't been back there since we were there. I've missed you so and I am such a jerk sometimes."

"I won't disagree with you on that point," Dorrie said laughing.

"And you are so perfect; Miss Dean's List; Miss Virgin; Miss Never Make a Mistake on Your Assignments;" Alex said sarcastically. "I am sending Allen at seven. Be ready." He dropped her arms and stormed out of her office, banging the door behind him.

She was ready and wearing a new dress she had recently purchased. She knew it showed off her figure and looked good. She strapped on some high heels and sprayed a new fragrance behind her ears and on her wrists. Allen arrived on time and drove her quietly to the Italian restaurant. The hostess recognized her and explained that Mr. Shingly had not arrived yet. Would she like to wait in their private room? She would. She ordered some wine and then another. She guessed she had been stood up. She called Allen and asked if he could pick her up, and he said he was on the way to her now.

Alex rushed into the room; looking frantic and disheveled. He ran his fingers through his hair and said,

"Oh, I was so scared, you would leave." He kissed her thoroughly. "I need a drink," he told the waiter, who hurried to comply. He also bought another wine for Dorrie. I am going to be smashed before this night is over, thought Dorrie.

Alex removed heavy documents from his inner jacket and dropped them in front of Dorrie. She picked them up gingerly and read them thoroughly. A large smile crossed her face and she flung herself into Alex's arms.

"Oh, thank you, thank you," she breathed, "you are the most wonderful boss in the whole world." She kissed him and then she hugged him. Alex thought he was going to fall to the floor and sat down heavily with her on his lap. The waiter brought the drinks and left quickly.

The papers were the deed to her building. The firm had bought the building. She was overjoyed and so grateful.

"I have one more item," he said. He handed her a single sheet of vellum. The top read "Quick Claim Deed." The firm had sold her the building for one dollar. Dorrie started to cry.

"Remind me to have Allen pick me up some more handkerchiefs," Alex said grumpily. "Shall we toast to your latest acquisition?"

Dorrie drank and ate and chattered endlessly. The more she drank, the more she talked. At one point Alex asked her what she wanted for Christmas and she told him she already had it, dancing around the room waving her deed wildly. She asked Alex what he wanted, but later she couldn't remember what he had said. She kissed him a thousand times and he seemed amused at her exuberance. She didn't remember getting home or who had put her to bed. She emerged from her bedroom holding her head and went to the bathroom to empty her stomach into the commode. She sat on the floor hugging the bowl and vomiting from time to time. Dorrie was sure she was going to die. "And I haven't even made a will to leave my beautiful building to someone." She thought sadly. "I'll leave it to Maureen," she said out loud and then threw up again.

The phone was ringing incessantly but Dorrie didn't move. Someone was banging on her door, so she pulled herself up, and went to answer. Maureen rushed in and gasped at Dorrie's disheveled condition.

"Oh my goodness," she said. "What did he do to you? I'll kill him. I'll hire a hit man. Who does he think he is – some high and mighty lawyer? What has he done to my poor baby?"

Maureen bustled around, cleaning up the mess, getting Dorrie into the bath and then into clean clothes; making tea; and finally settling down in the kitchen.

"Now," she demanded, "you tell me everything that happened."

Dorrie looked ashamed. "I got drunk," she said.

"Obviously," said Maureen wryly.

Dorrie started to cry. "He bought the building and gave it to me. I own this building and my great apartment and I got drunk and who knows what I said to him," a horrified look came over her face, "or what I let him do to me."

Maureen hugged her carefully and wiped her face with a napkin.

"Someone put me to bed," she whispered miserably.

Maureen rocked her gently; singing an old Irish lullaby over and over; and that was how Alex found them when he burst through the door.

"Why didn't you answer the phone?" he demanded. "I thought you were dead or worse." He added sheepishly, "Hi Maureen."

"Pshaw," Maureen said angrily. "When he's gone, call me at Lucinda's" she told Dorrie and slammed out the door.

"Ouch," said Dorrie, holding her head as the door slammed.

"Dorrie," Alex said gently, "you really tied one on last night. I feel responsible. I should have stopped you from drinking so much, but to tell the truth, I was drunker than you. Allen rescued us; dumped us into the car and took us home. At least I think he did. I woke up in my bed."

"Me too," said Dorrie. She jumped up and ran to the bathroom where she proceeded to puke. Alex bought her some aspirin and a cold compress for her head. He lifted her up and put her in her bed. She immediately fell asleep.

Chapter nine

Dorrie gave Maureen and Lucinda and her baby Jimmy presents for Christmas. She spent the day at Lucinda's house and walked home before dark.

She had left a Christmas card in Alex's mailbox. He sent her some flowers and a box of candy. She spent New Year's alone reading a book and going to bed early.

When school started in January, and since no one told her differently, she returned to her old schedule. The rhythm soothed her and she enjoyed solitary walks and visits with Maureen, Lucinda and Jimmy. They often lunched out, leaving Jimmy with his nanny.

Dorrie had contacted each tenant and explained she was the new landlord. She gave a musician on the first floor a notice to vacate and he went quietly; more quiet than his loud music. The tenant on her floor gave her notice and Dorrie decided she would not rent out that apartment, but would enlarge hers by making the two into one. Maureen found her a carpenter and when Dorrie was home she heard him singing dirty Irish ditties as he worked. Dorrie laughed.

Alex seldom saw Dorrie, but left her notes and files and a list of research he wanted performed. In July, Alex called her into his office and gave her a raise.

"I will be away all summer," Alex told her. "If there is an emergency, please tell Mrs. Greer as she has my itinerary. I believe you will be taking the Bar Exam in August and I would like to hear the results. You can take off as much time as you need to study or rest or," he hesitated, "or whatever." Dorrie thought he looked very tired. "Feel free to use Allen anytime you need a ride."

"Thank you," Dorrie said quietly and politely. "I do believe I will take a vacation also. I will give Mrs. Greer the dates."

Alex watched her go. "What went wrong?" he asked himself.

Dorrie took Maureen to Cape Cod for a week and they had a grand time shopping and swimming and laughing at silly jokes. Lucinda took care of the boarding house, but there was only one boarder left and Maureen hoped he would leave soon. She was tired and wanted to spend more time with Jimmy.

When she returned home, she threw herself into preparation for the Bar Exam and when it was over, waited impatiently for the results.

Alex returned from his extended vacation looking tanned. He had lost weight and ordered new suits which he asked Dorrie to pick up, using Allen for transportation. He got into the practice of stopping by Dorrie's office and asking her to accompany him to court. She loved the atmosphere and spent her time examining what Alex did to make him such a successful lawyer. She made some shy suggestions on occasion and Alex appeared to really approve of her ideas. There was no personal interaction and Dorrie missed it.

"I really love him," she thought, one lonely night. "I really made a mistake." She was much more sophisticated now. "Older and wiser," she thought.

Alex called her into his office one Friday afternoon. "I have the results of your Bar Exam here. I do NOT want any crying. You can always repeat it."

Dorrie's heart sank. She hadn't passed. She took the envelope from him and opened it slowly. Tears came to her eyes.

"I said no crying," Alex said sternly.

"But these are tears of joy," she said choking on her words, "because I made it. I made it. Oh thank heavens, I made it." She sat down stunned.

"Allen will pick you up at seven," Alex said, "Go home and get pretty. We are going to celebrate."

Dorrie left by the back door and Allen was waiting.

"Congratulations," he said. It wasn't until later that Dorrie wondered how he knew so soon.

At seven he rang her doorbell; always prompt; always attentive.

"I wish I could find someone like Allen," she thought sadly.

Allen drove her to a fancy hotel in Copley Square and the door man directed her upstairs to "the first room on the left."

"This can't be right," thought Dorrie. She was about to turn, when she saw Maureen coming out of the ladies room.

"What are you doing here?" asked Dorrie.

Maureen didn't answer her but opened the door and shoved Dorrie inside.

"Congratulations, congratulations," yelled the people inside. Alex came to her side and led her to the front of the room. Dorrie was stunned. Alex made a short speech and Mrs. Greer actually hugged her. The room was filled with lawyers and judges and even Allen and his wife were there.

All the secretaries from the pool were present and there was a band and drinks and food and sloppy congratulations. The evening was spectacular and after a few drinks Dorrie had tears in her eyes.

"Do not cry," Alex whispered in her ear. "Don't you dare cry. I went to a lot of work to pull this off and you cannot cry!"

Alex's mother Mary came and hugged her. "I am very proud of you." She said.

Alex and Dorrie danced often and he held her close, looking deeply into her eyes. "Oh, Alex," she thought. "I really do love you." She didn't say it out loud.

Dorrie danced with everyone and accepted cards and presents from so many of the people she lost track. Maureen and Lucinda hugged her several times.

The party appeared to be winding down and Alex stood, banging his glass with his spoon.

"Dorrie," he said nervously. "Please come here."

Everyone gathered in a circle and the talking died down.

When Dorrie approached, she noticed how pale he was. "I hope he isn't sick" she thought. Alex took both her hands in his and gazed into her eyes. Releasing one of hands, he put his hand in his pocket, went down on one knee and produced a spectacular engagement ring.

"Doreen Eleanor Dustin, will you please do me the honor of becoming my wife?"

Dorrie was speechless. Alex stood and took her hand, placing the ring on her third finger. He drew her to him and kissed her thoroughly.   The room erupted in cheers and hurrahs and loud banter.

"You had better say yes," Alex whispered.   "I am going to feel damn silly if you don't."

"Oh yes," said Dorrie, "oh yes, my darling."   And she kissed him thoroughly.

THE END

Dorrie sat at her desk. May's head popped up again. "Are you okay?"

"I'm fine," Dorrie answered miserably.

Mrs. Greer arrived at her desk with several files and explained carefully what she wanted done with each of them. Dorrie took notes efficiently.

Mrs. Greer put her hand on Dorrie's shoulder and said, "Don't be upset. Alex can be a bear; especially in the middle of a big trial. He didn't know you are a genius as a typist."

Dorrie got busy on the new files; noting they were for a different lawyer and wondered who he was and what he was like. A shadow fell across her desk and she looked up apprehensively. Mr. Shingly held out his hand and said "Truce?"

Dorrie nodded and shook his hand firmly.